BLOOD BRANDED

BOOK ONE OF
THE MIX-BLOOD
SERIES

J.A. ALEXSOO

BLOOD BRANDED

BOOK ONE OF
THE MIX-BLOOD
SERIES

BREEZY PAGES

The Mix-Blood: Book One
BLOOD BRANDED

ISBN:
    978-0-9952378-4-1 (paperback)
    978-0-9952378-6-5 (kindle edition)

First Printing: October 2019
    Map by Tad Davis
    Cover by Hugh Pindur
    Editing by David Antrobus

Published by Breezy Pages Publishing

Visit: **www.JAAlexsoo.com**

In loving memory of the best dad
Miss you every day

N
W
E
S
2018
HAMMERSTONE
© J.A. ALEXSOO - 2018

WHERE THERE'S SMOKE...

Thick smoke soiled the air. Orcs clashed with red-smeared weapons. Roars of triumph and pain assaulted the senses, mingling with the scent of blood. Dry grass burned around stone structures, spreading like wildfire.

The gray orc slashed another crimson in his way. An arrow bit into his leg; he growled and limped to an unfinished tower with little cover. The grayback fell when the next arrow found his back. He crawled to a cage of frantic pigeons, pulling on the latch. The cage door swung open and he attached a rolled up note to one of the pigeons before slumping to the dirt.

Master Valrix lowered her bow; a malicious grin spread across her delicate human face. The sun snuck through the smoke as the birds took flight.

"We can follow..." the prime crimson said but trailed off when his master readied another shot.

Dark energy swirled around the arrow before she released it. Shadow duplicates accompanied the projectile, homing in on the escaping vermin. Master Valrix walked through the ash and feathers that drifted down from the sky. She stopped where the parchment had fallen from its courier and scooped up the singed letter.

H. They're coming, it read.

"The last of the grays are herded," the prime reported.

"Good," Valrix sneered. "We head east. Tribute season is upon us."

She crumpled the paper and threw it into the open flames. The parchment caught fire, and a horde of crimsons and their new grayback slaves marched from the sacked settlement, the new beginning the grays had hoped for now a smoking ruin.

Stupid fools.

The prime eyed the burning message with growing anticipation, watching the creeping flames devour it, right up to the first mark. The source of the meddling grays.

Hammerstone.

PROLOGUE

MIX-BLOOD

I have to win."

The words pierced the chatter among the gathering, reaching Frafnar and echoing his own thoughts.

"I want to see a crimson!" another hollered.

"Better hope you're not against me!" someone else shouted.

Then the energy of the group stilled as if everyone held their breath. Frafnar stood on the tips of his toes, but he still couldn't see past the bobbing heads and shoulders of the other runts.

"Frafnar, son of Armastus."

His elation was cut short by the groans of the group. The outbursts ceased when Trainer Groth roared for silence.

"His opponent will be..."

The gathering leaned forward.

"Bromh, son of—"

"No!" Bromh yelled from within the crowd. "I won't be paired against the mix-blood."

"Then you forfeit," Groth said, already searching for the next contender.

"I never said—"

"Get over here," Groth snapped. "Where's Frafnar? Let him through."

The circle of bodies parted enough that Frafnar squeezed between them, ignoring the sharp stares from the others. He kept his chin high and broke eye contact only as he passed the runts towering over him.

Trainer Groth and Bromh waited in the center of the ring.

"What's the matter?" Frafnar taunted when he broke through the crowd. "Afraid you'll lose?"

Bromh scoffed. "I'll crush you in an instant, twig."

Groth's scowl deepened. Veins popped out of the tight flesh on his arms and neck.

"Fine," Bromh stammered. "But everyone knows I should've had a real challenge," he dared to add.

"Get into position."

Frafnar met Bromh in the middle of the circle, a solid wood construction between them.

"Winner moves on to the finals," Groth reiterated with a huff.

Frafnar mirrored Bromh by grasping the iron bar on the side of the wood platform with one hand and placing his elbow on the leather pad. Bromh glared over their clasped hands and squeezed so hard his knuckles paled. Maybe when he was younger, Frafnar might have cried out because of the pain. Today, Bromh would have to break his hand before he'd let go. When he won, they'd have no choice but to acknowledge him as an orc.

Trainer Groth balanced two thin strips of kindling on each side of their hands to ensure they started at his command. "Prepare," he said. Then, after a suspense-filled moment, "Go."

The audience erupted with noise, hollering as the strips fell over. Frafnar met Bromh's strength with his own. He inched his opponent's arm halfway down to the wood surface. The notion of a quick triumph crumbled when he heard Bromh snicker.

"That all you got, twig?"

The force against Frafnar's arm intensified, and he barely slowed the progress of their hands moving in the opposite direction of his goal. Bromh was toying with him. Prolonging victory to watch him squirm.

He couldn't let him win!

Frafnar felt the power build inside him before he made the conscious decision, spreading out and enhancing his abilities. There was no discernible sign of magic; maybe they wouldn't notice.

Bromh pushed for one final surge to finish it. Frafnar's hand hovered over the wood but wouldn't fall. Confusion then rage replaced the confidence in Bromh's eyes as Frafnar reclaimed the upper hand. Bromh roared in protest when Frafnar slammed his arm down.

The ensuing silence made Frafnar focus on those gathered around them, who stared with mouths gaping.

"Winner: Frafnar," Trainer Groth announced.

"Cheater!" Bromh pointed. "He used magic."

A pit formed in Frafnar's stomach.

Groth frowned. "I saw nothing."

"A mix-blood won, he must have—"

"Even if he did," Groth said, "there's no rule against it. The outcome remains the same." He turned to Frafnar, who'd barely had a moment to bask in victory. "Who will take your place in the final selection?"

Frafnar blinked. "What?"

Annoyance was thick in the trainer's voice, as if it were obvious. "Only pure-blooded orcs join the tribute excursions to the crimson border."

"It should be *me*. You're a cheating twig," Bromh said.

Frafnar felt desperation swell inside him. "I won the right to move on to the finals... the chance to defend the tribute like my father."

Groth answered with a flat stare. "Choose."

Frafnar clenched his fists and shook his head as he shoved his way back through the crowd.

Bromh's voice followed, shaking with fury. "I hope the crimsons kill you."

The axe fell.

A satisfying crack filled the air as the metal bit as deep as it would go. Frafnar pulled back, working the handle until the axe came loose. He struck again, and again. His muscles burned, and he felt the sting of popped blisters, but he didn't stop. He tore through blocks of wood as if they were real enemies, dropping them at his feet.

Frafnar ignored the whispers, even as they intensified at times, like waves beating against a rocky shore. He hated them. They also thought he was weak. His axe jammed again, and when he couldn't rip it free this time, the whispers swarmed him.

They're coming for you.

"Go away!" Frafnar tossed the axe—wood attached—as far as he could. It landed several feet away, causing a nearby squirrel to jabber and flick its tail emphatically before darting behind a tree.

Frafnar wiped the sweat from his face. The whispers fell

silent, and the rage inside simmered. Two swift horn calls in the distance froze him.

"He's back."

He stacked the chopped pieces of wood in his arms and headed back to Hammerstone, toward the south side-gate that was positioned between the back end of the trade and common areas. The outer stone walls of the settlement guided him to the entrance, an unnecessary line of defense in his opinion. What was it to protect them from? A horde of roaming monsters or a mob of dissatisfied merchants? He'd never met either one. Neither had he ever seen a crimson. Maybe they would never come.

When Frafnar reached the gate, the orc on watch barely offered him a glance. The guard kept his weapon close and his eyes peeled on the forest. Why was everyone on edge at this time of year? It wasn't like the crimsons ever ventured this deep into grayback territory. The stories about their orc cousins did nothing to quench his desire to see them first-hand. While lost in his imaginings, he was yanked back to reality with a single word.

"Twig."

Boisterous laughter filled the air from the group of runts approaching from the opposite direction. Bromh led them, the biggest of his company, even larger than his siblings.

Frafnar stiffened but stayed his course. As Bromh passed, he shoulder-slammed Frafnar, who was ready for it, until one of the others shoved him. Despite his stumble, Frafnar managed to keep his grip on the wood. Foul names were launched from the group as they turned and trailed him. They'd wait until it was safe to jump him, when no adults were around.

It took all of Frafnar's willpower to keep walking and not merely curse back at them. His emotions fueled the heat in his words, and he did not realize the power in them until it was too late. He half expected an explosion or something of the sort. When nothing like that happened, he burst out laughing at the sight of the offending runts.

The group stopped and looked down. Their clothes had been replaced with white-and-red-dotted short leggings. Bromh shot him a fierce glare, and Frafnar bolted.

"You're dead!"

A TYPICAL DAY

Cursing chased Frafnar as he dashed past orcs and through the practically vacant market. The blocks of wood remained securely in his arms as he raced away.

He had to make it home. They wouldn't dare bother him there. Frafnar made a detour when a couple of them tried to cut off his escape. He darted around every corner and finally ducked behind a stack of crates. The edge of the Dwellings wasn't far.

A whistle squashed his smidgen of hope. The warning would alert the others that he'd been spotted, so he fled from the direction of the sound. Frafnar rushed down an alley, entering a large open area between buildings. Sunlight squeezed above the roofs, exposing the laundry to warmth as it shifted in the breeze. Bedclothes hung from ropes that stretched the width of the alleyway. Since he'd grown up with it, the sight wasn't unusual to him, but the adults told stories of a different way of life before Hammerstone.

Sounds of pursuit pushed Frafnar into the rows of

sheets. By the time he reached the end, shouts erupted behind him as the others tangled in the obstacles. He was jogging down a narrow lane between dwellings when he stumbled on another runt searching for him at the next intersection. Fortunately, he was searching in the opposite direction, and Frafnar had time to scramble into the shadows of an alcove. The runts behind him were closing in, but he had a plan. He stayed put for a couple breaths then risked a peek.

No one had eyes on him for the moment. He threw one of his pieces of wood farther down the alley. At this rate, he might make it home without a beating. How many were ahead of him now? His best chance would be to get behind all of them so he could slip away and find another route home. He refused to face his father with a bruised and bloodied body—the fate of a loser. A weakling. A mix-blood.

Frafnar flattened himself against the wall of the alcove as best he could.

"This way! He went down here."

A couple of figures ran past him, and a few more followed soon after. The sound of their footfalls faded into the distance, so he emerged and collected the piece of wood. He flipped it once before reuniting the block with the pile clutched beneath his other arm.

Frafnar backtracked to the end of the alleyway that led to the cloth-drying area. Seconds later, Bromh came speeding around the corner. Frafnar ducked, and Bromh spilled over him. Escape was no longer an option when he felt a hand wrap around his ankle.

"Gotcha."

3

ROUGH-AND-TUMBLE

Chaos reigned as a flurry of elbows, kicks, shouts, and grunts filled Frafnar's world.

Bromh was in the middle of alerting his gang with a whistle when Frafnar silenced him with a foot to the face. Bromh snarled, and the scuffle continued until the others found them. After overpowering Frafnar the ruffians dragged him down an empty alley in case the fighting had attracted attention.

Frafnar locked his muscles and tried to shake them off, but too many held him. They threw him to the ground and gathered in a circle.

"Call for help," one of them said through gritted teeth. "I dare ya."

Frafnar's reply was cut short as the onslaught of kicks began. At first he tried to fight back, but inevitably he had to use his arms to block some of the brutal blows.

The ringleader arrived and pushed his cronies aside. He

grabbed Frafnar by the neck then hoisted him to his feet. Frafnar noticed the blood on Bromh's lip, and he cracked a triumphant grin.

"Let's see how much you smile when I knock your teeth out," Bromh said while his friends restrained their quarry.

"Can't fight me by yourself? Afraid you'll lose to a mix-blood again?" Frafnar spat red into Bromh's face.

The whispers returned as Bromh drew back his arm, fist clenched for the strike. Reflex tempted Frafnar to close his eyes, but he resisted the urge, just as he resisted the demons. And so, he was as surprised as all of them when a ball of packed snow exploded against the back of Bromh's head, who staggered from the blow and wiped the wet snow from his ear.

"Tricks won't save you, twig." Bromh pulled back his arm again, but this time the air filled with a shower of fist-sized snowballs that pelted down on the runts.

Frafnar felt the magic in it, as one perceives mist in the early morning. Maybe it was luck that he avoided the ice, or something else, but he'd take advantage of the distraction.

The snow was harmless, but the group instinctively covered their heads and shouted in protest. Frafnar shut his eyes and concentrated on the weave of magic. He tugged on it, molding a part of it to his design. They couldn't say he'd cheated; it wasn't his magic. It could only be—

The snow at their feet transformed into a thick sheet of ice, and the group tumbled to the ground, Frafnar included. The ruffians lost their grip, and he was able to untangle himself before they could nab him again. He pushed off one of the flailing bodies and slid from the slick surface to solid ground. With this chance to escape, Frafnar took off running, but as he rounded a corner he slammed into someone, which landed him back on the cobblestones. He was expecting to be pounced on again, but instead, a human woman stared down at him.

"Eema!"

4

___

EEMA

The sounds of the runts escaping the ice drove Frafnar to his feet to stand beside—not behind, never behind—the woman, whose gaze swung to his pursuers as they came into sight.

The group bumped into each other as they stopped upon seeing her, dressed in light fur and leather armor with hands on her hips. She raised her index finger and stepped forward, but before she could take a breath the runts scattered.

"Run! Before the Pale Witch turns us into slugs," one of them yelled.

"If only it were that easy," Sera murmured.

Bromh glowered at Frafnar as he backed up. Of course, he'd see Frafnar's good fortune as a coward's escape. His glare voiced his unspoken words. *Your Eema can't save you forever.*

Sera sighed. "That was close... who started it this time?"

"Why did you help? I didn't ask for any."

His mother arched an eyebrow. "You didn't have to. I've told you: you don't have to be like them. There are different kinds of strength."

Frafnar turned away and rolled his eyes as she continued to spout on about stubborn pigheaded orcs, a point of view he'd heard many times when she argued with his father.

"Anyway." She cleared her throat. "How did you use gritt to change my snow into ice?"

"It just happened," Frafnar lied. "I don't know how."

Mistaking his nervousness for embarrassment, her face beamed with misplaced understanding. "You can master it! Let's try again when we get home."

Home, Frafnar thought. It felt like days since he'd been there.

A final horn blast echoed from the main gate of the settlement. Sera paused to listen. "Let's get moving. Your father won't stay long."

They backtracked to where he'd dropped the wood during the scuffle. It took little time to collect it. He couldn't help but drag his feet while they weaved their way through the maze of dwellings, kicking loose stones that had the misfortune of crossing his path.

"Dejara told me she'd sent you for wood—" She fell silent when she realized he'd fallen behind. "Fraf?" She stayed quiet until he caught up. "You're still angry? I know you want to go with your father on his missions, but..."

Frafnar made no effort to confirm it, but somehow she knew. He didn't flinch when she touched his shoulder, a part of him secretly hoping she'd offer one of her infamous hugs. She didn't. Probably for the best.

"He can't take you," she continued. "The inner settlements would betray us—"

Frafnar bristled. "I know."

5

STRENGTH IN BLOOD

It didn't take long for Frafnar to pile the wood in the storeroom, and after he finished he went to follow his mother inside. Before he entered he heard muffled voices and paused to identify them. Had his father returned?

His hand hovered above the latch while he paused to distinguish who was speaking; one was obviously his mother. The door opened from inside, revealing him poised for a latch that was no longer in reach.

Dejara stood in the entrance, looking over her shoulder. "Don't take long, Sera. We need you on the wall." Her long braids swung as she turned to leave, almost barreling through him before stopping short. "Frafnar. There you are. I hear the wood is restocked despite some trouble. We'll make an orc of you yet."

She ruffled the top of his head and walked past. "Was that the correct action?" she called back and cocked an ear for the response.

"Yep." Sera's voice carried from inside. "But you could try to hug your nephew at least once."

Dejara blanched. "You humans and your hugs and handshakes. A strong-arm punch says it all," she mumbled half under her breath and set out.

Sera was inspecting her shield when Frafnar finally crossed the threshold.

"Your father will be home soon. Do you want to practice altering magic before he arrives?"

The spark of hope in her eyes forced Frafnar to suppress a groan. Reluctantly, he knelt with her on the pelt-covered floor. A small flame sparked to life and floated above Sera's open palm.

"Okay, Fraf, you know what to do."

Valrix fiddled with the twig between her fingers while studying the roughly drawn map in the dirt. As far as she could tell, her army had obliterated Hammerstone's allies. They were alone and isolated. Valrix snapped the twig in half.

She crouched and idly plucked more sticks from near her feet. Scouting from the air had revealed much. Of particular interest was the hidden magical barrier around the settlement that foiled her plans of dropping a surprise assault. If it was removed, the arcane blast wouldn't kill the grays, but the flying debris and collapsed buildings might well do so.

Fortunately, her excursion appeared to have gone unnoticed. Demonic or not, this unanticipated obstacle would make for a much more interesting fight. Valrix squeezed the bundle of sticks in her hands. A mere twist of her wrists cracked the wood apart.

With enough force, anything will break.

The crimson orcs shifted restlessly around her. It wasn't her actions that caused their unease but rather the waiting for what was to come. They would obey or die.

None spoke except for the prime orc, her second, who prattled on in a low tone next to her, describing the layout as if she were a blind fool.

"It doesn't matter which wall or gate. Are they in place yet?" she asked, her impatience mounting.

"No word yet," the prime answered.

"Be sure the horde remains back far enough that they won't be detected until it's time to attack, or it'll be your head."

The prime nodded, accustomed to her threats. "We can strike as soon as they're ready."

Valrix resisted the urge to hit the bald orc, but she too had her orders. "I didn't ask for your opinion. You will do as I command."

"Of course," the prime knelt, his mass of bulging muscles an impressive sight compared to the thin human vessel of the demose. "But the tribute will still be ours if we attack first."

This pestering would never happen if my vessel had been a Remnent rather than a simple sorcerer, the demon thought within Valrix.

She offered no warning before planting a foot on the prime's face and kicking off. The crimson fell back, but there was a blur of movement, and an invisible bulk broke his fall.

The figure of a giant ghostly wolf materialized. Its head swung back at the orc who leaned against its mass, snout wrinkled, and fiendish teeth bared. Fear was rare to behold in orc eyes, and Valrix enjoyed every moment of it.

The prime slid to the ground on his knees, head bent in submission. Blood dripped freely from his nose. Valrix sensed the swelling of energy from the gathering of crimsons, like a sharp intake of breath that was ready to burst. With one chilling look from the demon, the tension subsided like a long exhale.

"Strength in blood," one orc said.

In unison, the rest repeated the words and returned to their boredom.

Valrix stroked the wolf's side. "Take the pack and surround Hammerstone. Remain hidden, but kill any grays that try to escape."

The wolf snorted before it vanished into the woods, followed by a ghostly pack.

Valrix focused on the prime at her feet. "We wait."

He nodded, and she basked in satisfying silence.

HOME

You can do it."

His mother's words were soft and full of encouragement as Frafnar studied the flame hovering above her palm. To practice gritt, he needed to either mold her magic to his will or snuff it out entirely. If he could, he might have to leave his home to be with the Avant Guard knights in some strange land. The prospect made his stomach flip.

Frafnar played with the flame, forcing it to burn bright then dwindle until it was the size of a pebble, but never altering it completely. He held back, his mind reeling with doubt. Why did she want him to go if he had gritt? The demose were annoying but nothing more.

She thinks you're weak.

His temper flared.

"I can't!" Frafnar scrambled to his feet and climbed the short ladder to his balcony and loft. He slammed his door for effect but stayed outside and flattened himself on the floor.

He quietly crawled to the banister and peeked over the edge.

His mother continued to stare at the flame, calm as always despite his brash ways. Her eyes looked distant, as though she were lost in thought. She folded her fingers over her palm, and the fire died in a puff of smoke.

A shuffling at the door caused her to reach for her weapon, but she relaxed as it creaked open. Frafnar couldn't see the door from his vantage point, but he imagined the large figure that filled most of the entrance.

"Expecting trouble?" a familiar voice asked.

Sera's features softened. "The good kind." She moved toward the opening and out of sight.

It took several silent moments before she walked back into view, now accompanied by his father. "Dejara said you were holding my supplies hostage unless I claimed them myself," Armastus said while eyeing the items in the corner.

"Can you blame me?" A mischievous grin played at the corners of Sera's mouth.

Armastus untangled himself from her to restock the sack resting on his shoulder. "The crimsons won't tolerate late payment."

Sera rested her hands on her hips, her leather creaking. "The tribute will leave when it's ready, and you can catch up." She sighed. "Do you know he's still upset?"

"Who?"

"You know very well who."

Armastus paused in the middle of placing another item in his pack. "Where is he?"

Frafnar slid away from sight before searching eyes could spot him.

"Can he not travel with you some of the way?"

His father's voice had an edge to it but didn't rise in volume. "No."

Frafnar clenched his fist. If the crimsons discovered Hammerstone's changes from the permitted norm—the acceptance of mix-breeds included—their rebellion would be crushed.

"Others of his age weren't picked, even those bigger than him," Armastus continued. "He must accept it."

"Size isn't everything." Frafnar detected the pride in his mother's tone.

His father's chuckle was deep. "You've proven that."

Frafnar risked a peek again and saw his father had resumed packing. Sera's hands rested on the back of a chair while she watched. Her fingers drummed against the wood.

"Say what's on your mind, woman."

Sera straightened and clasped her hands behind her back. "Our son used gritt again today. Accident or not, I still think I should take him to the Order."

Frafnar shook his head. He dared not blink and miss his father's response.

THE HORN

Armastus yanked the lacing so hard when closing his pack that Frafnar was surprised it didn't snap. "We haven't done all this to let them have him."

Sera didn't appear concerned. "The Order can help him far better than I can."

"Your instruction will be enough."

"This is serious! The crimsons could come any season now, and he'd be safer with the knights. If a demose corrupts him—" The rest of Sera's words fell unspoken as a horn call warned them that the tribute of goods was leaving. She glared out the window as though the sound had favored Armastus in the discussion.

"He's strong. He belongs here," Armastus said with renewed calm, hoisting the supplies over his shoulder.

"Be careful."

Sera's words made Armastus stop halfway to the door. He returned to her and kissed her forehead. "Protect them."

His mother took the opportunity to tug on his father's

collar and whisper in his ear. Frafnar strained to hear, but his father's laughter filled the room.

"Stubborn woman. Fine, we'll wrestle for it—when I get back."

There was an eagerness in Sera's eyes as Armastus left. She whistled a tune and collected her things. Frafnar ducked out of sight again. He heard her footsteps halt below.

"Fraf, I must go. Stay here, or you can join me on the wall." She waited, but he remained silent. "I'll be at the main gate if you change your mind."

After he heard the door close, Frafnar slid back to the edge of the balcony and rested his chin on his hands. Light streamed in through the window, and dust floated in the air while he contemplated what to do. He visually scoured the contents of the dwelling as if searching for the answer. An unexpected item gripped his attention. His father's horn.

He sat up. Had it been forgotten by accident... or on purpose? Either way, it took him only a split second to make up his mind. It took the same amount of time for him to jump to his feet and enter his room to fetch the newly repaired weapon he'd made. His mother had forbidden him from using the slingshot against the other runts, but it could be useful to guard the tribute! He fastened it to his belt beside his bag of stones. Frafnar dropped from the balcony and rushed over to the horn. He slid his fingers over the engraved designs before securing the leather strap over his shoulder.

Unwilling to waste any more time, Frafnar flung himself out the front door and straight into a mountain of papers and books balanced precariously on two legs. Too late to stop, he collided with a whirlwind of crinkling parchment.

The man hit the ground among a rain of documents. If the human had been an orc, Frafnar would be the one off his feet. The man straightened the specs on his nose.

"Fraf—wha—?"

"Sorry, Erik." Frafnar darted through the carnage and backpedaled away. "Father forgot his horn."

"I'm supposed to..." his uncle began, but then realizing the mess around him, his shoulders slumped. "Oh no."

8

———

THE GATE

Frafnar had to leave before sundown. A quick inspection of the horn reassured him that it had survived the collision with his uncle. He raced past buildings and orcs alike toward the north side-gate. Armed with his slingshot, he wasn't concerned about running into the other runts. The moment Frafnar caught sight of the gate he thought he was in the clear, but he nearly knocked over a stack of supplies when his aunt walked into view.

Dejara approached the guard stationed outside the gate. "How goes?"

"All are back. The straw and oil barriers are finished," he answered. "Were you not on the main gate?"

Dejara flashed him a faint smile. "Someone has to be here when you're out."

She headed back under the gate, raised a hand, and dropped it forward. The sound of clinking chains and the screech of metal made Frafnar's gut wrench. He glanced at the sky.

No! It was too early. Why were they closing the gate so soon?

Dejara was chatting with a passerby some distance away by the time the gate was halfway down. Her back finally turned, and Frafnar sprang at the chance. The noise of his sprint was buried in the groaning of metal and wood as the gate continued to descend.

The spikes on the bottom metal bar were already lowered to a level that forced Frafnar to hold the horn as he rolled through. Before hiding behind the wall, he glimpsed Dejara turning toward the portcullis as it touched down. He waited for a few heartbeats, then fist-pumped the air with the horn in triumph.

That was close. If his aunt caught sight of him, she'd drag him back. He sighed, then realized that a guard was watching him from the base of the wall with a puzzled stare.

"Armastus forgot his horn..." Frafnar blurted the one thing that might save him from being marched home.

The guard rolled his eyes. "When he sends you back, make yourself useful and keep watch in one of the empty towers until daybreak," he said before heading off to his station.

Frafnar exhaled, ready to yell a smart reply until he remembered Dejara wasn't far. He clamped his jaw shut and left in the direction of the road.

9

———

A LOUD CRASH

Y ou shouldn't be here."

The old man raised his chin defiantly in response to Armastus. "I'm not afraid. I've been trading with Hammerstone for years now." He rubbed his shoulder from trying to get the wheel back on the cart himself before Armastus had arrived. "My sons didn't want me to come. They think I'm frail and old—shows them wrong."

Perplexed, Armastus fastened the wheel back on the man's cart with ease. "Trade season is over," he answered more loudly.

"Hogwash. We never miss it, do we, Betty?"

Armastus raised an eyebrow then realized the man was addressing the mule, who merely exhaled heavily. One last kick guaranteed the wheel was firmly attached to the cart. The blanket covering the mound of apples had saved most of the fruit from escaping during the crash, but Armastus spied a stray one near his feet and bent to get it.

The human clicked his tongue, and the cart creaked forward with Betty diligently leading the way.

"Whoa there." Two large strides allowed Armastus to catch up and pull back on the reins.

Betty wouldn't be deterred. Even when Armastus pulled harder, she dipped her head and pressed on.

"When she sets her mind on something…" the human began but stopped when Armastus held the apple under the mule's nose.

The cart stopped, and Betty's ears perked up. Her eyes grew almost as round as her nostrils that inhaled the sweet scent of fruit. A sharp smack joined the noise of Betty's munching. Armastus narrowed his eyes at the cane that rested where it had assaulted his arm, then up at the owner.

"Hands off," the human said, glaring back.

"I fixed your wheel, now go home." Armastus pointed south.

The human glanced over his shoulder then shook his head. "No. I have these here apples to trade. I have the same right as anyone."

As if in agreement, Betty finished her snack and nearly removed Armastus's fingers with the last bite. The human jerked with surprise when Armastus yanked on the cane and snapped the wooden shaft in half.

Betty's head bobbed upward in alarm, and the cart lurched forward. The old human lifted a wooden panel next to his seat and retrieved a new cane, pointing it at the sky. "Many more where that came from, my boy. I'm no stranger to orc tempers. I came prepared."

Fed up and short on time, Armastus was ready to call someone else to deal with the infuriating human. After searching his waist, the absence of the horn sent a wave of mixed emotions through him—a fiery rage tempered by icy panic.

"Damn that woman."

The nearest lookout was too far to be of use. It was the north road they now watched carefully, not the south. He could forget his horn, borrow one from a lookout on his way to the tribute, and send the lookout to deal with the human.

But his pride overrode his reasoning.

Armastus sighed. No, it was best if he handled it himself. As much as their dealings with human farmers and roaming merchants had improved over the years, it wasn't worth risking their hard-earned reputation.

No sooner had Armastus reached a decision than the rear door on the rickety cart fell open. A river of apples spilled out onto the road. The human journeyed on, oblivious. Armastus breathed deeply, imagining throttling him. He scooped up an apple and threw it, hard. "Old man!"

The fruit slammed against the human's back. "Hey, no need to... dog-dang-it, the apples escaped again." He pulled on the reins. "Betty, whoa! And you stay right there. Don't you eat them all."

Armastus began to collect the fruit, already regretting his choice. "Next season, use barrels."

FIRST BLOOD

They think they're so clever, Master Valrix thought, utterly amused as she studied the company of graybacks who escorted the tribute.

Signal horns were counted among the group's inventory, some dangling casually from belts, resting on shoulders, or held in hand. They would never expect an attack so close to home during tribute season.

The prime next to her received a silent signal. "They're in place," he informed her, keeping his voice low.

Valrix smirked. Death would rain down heavily on the horn bearers.

Her horde waited as the graybacks drew closer on the road, the tension mounting when the company passed between the crimson groups hidden in the forest. Grayback voices carried through the woods, and Valrix cocked an arrow.

"Armastus is late."

Trainer Groth spat, uninterested.

The younger gray didn't seem concerned about Groth's reaction. "The Pale Witch must be some mate to—"

"Keep watch," Groth ordered. If the young ones felt they could speak with him, perhaps accustomed to his gruff nature, he'd have to up his game. He was in the middle of planning merciless training drills while the other gray blabbered on.

"I didn't think you'd join the tribute this season. You're getting old, Groth."

The idiot was lucky they'd left Hammerstone, or Groth would've shown him the definition of vigor with a punch to the jaw. Instead, he answered, "The hazards of a dull life. Perhaps the crimsons will see fit to kill us this time."

"I hope they try." The young gray's eagerness revealed his large canine teeth. "I'd love to challenge those sucklings."

Groth tuned out most of the orc's subsequent prattle until he mentioned relieving himself. "You can't break rank..."

The nitwit stopped at the side of the road, Groth on his heels. The tribute company didn't slow their pace westward.

"You should've handled this before we left!" Groth bellowed. "When the unit walks, you walk. When it stops, you stop."

"Hold this." The gray tossed his signal horn to Groth over his shoulder.

Groth stepped toward the orc, ready to pummel those deaf ears, but pain sliced across the side of his neck and staggered him. The gray fell over, an arrow shaft embedded in his skull. Groth turned in time to hear the click of crossbows and see those carrying signal horns struck down. Crimson orcs roared from the tree line and rushed the tribute group.

Ignoring the blood that flowed freely from his flesh wound, Groth took three strides toward the battle before he spied the human emerge from hiding. She released an arrow in his direction, and he batted it away with his arm buckler. The arrow snapped apart from the impact, but a searing pain worked its way up to his shoulder. It wasn't broken, but it felt like it nearly had been. The dent in his buckler confirmed the sheer force it had repelled.

Groth almost dropped the horn in anger, but its presence was a reminder of what he must do. Regret plagued him as he witnessed his people clash with the crimsons, but his grip tightened on the horn.

The human woman drew back another arrow, and Groth could see the red of her eyes. His arm throbbed. She was no mere human then.

She let loose, and Groth darted for the forest, cursing all the way. The arrow pierced the ground near his feet, throwing up dust. In the woods, he heard bark break and crack as he used the trees for cover.

Slipping away was his only option, or he'd be choking on his own blood before he could get a breath into the damn horn.

INTERCEPT

H e won't get far," the prime vowed as they lost sight of the grayback through the trees. After he gestured to where Groth had disappeared, a pair of crimsons broke off from the tribute and raced after their quarry.

Master Valrix redirected her aim from the forest to the battling orcs. A grayback's war cry weakened into a bloody garble when her arrow pierced his back.

"The warriors are in position. They'll stop him," the prime added, a slight tremble in his voice.

"They will"—Valrix drew back another arrow—"before he uses that horn..." She let it loose. "Or..."

The prime watched as her arrow found its mark in a gray's throat, emphasizing the threat.

When Frafnar neared an occupied watchtower—a rickety wooden structure—that guarded the southern length of the north road, he remembered to offer a whistle to announce himself.

The grayback's head peeked over the side as Frafnar passed and disappeared just as quick. Someone approaching from Hammerstone wouldn't be of concern to the lookout, but Frafnar wanted to avoid any more setbacks.

There was no sign of his father when he came to the road. Certain that there was little chance of getting there before him, Frafnar considered a more direct route through the woods to reach the tribute. The road was an easier run, but longer. The cool shade of the trees tempted him as he squinted in the late sun.

The tribute was probably a fair distance westward by now, both a blessing and a curse. Maybe they wouldn't tell him to return home. Either way, time was of the essence. Frafnar plunged into the forest, navigating the uneven ground, lunging from boulders and traversing fallen trees. At one point he passed an abandoned watchtower. The cracked wood was warped with age and looked ready to collapse. It was likely one of the first towers built when Hammerstone was founded, before the road was made.

With no time to dwell on it, he hustled by. He surged past endless columns of thick trunks, tearing himself free of bushes and foliage that clung and scratched him.

After a time, Frafnar stopped and bent over, hands on his knees. The road was farther than he'd thought. The setting sun dropped lower through the trees as he caught his breath, and he nearly leaped out of his skin when Trainer Groth appeared, bounding toward him at a mad run.

12

—————

BULLIES

G roth lifted the horn to his mouth. Before he could make the warning call, a crossbow bolt sliced Groth's side and he roared with rage. Frafnar could only stare as Groth rushed past him, knocking him down into the dense bushes.

From the ground, Frafnar saw Groth veer right. He was well ahead of the ones who sent the bolts when a colossal shadow dropped from a tree. Groth disentangled himself from his new assailant and rose to his feet, a foot shorter than his enemy with bloodred skin.

Frafnar's jaw dropped. A crimson—a real crimson!

Despite his opponent's enormous size, Groth lunged, fists leading. Frafnar's initial excitement soured to panic as the two fought. Groth's hits didn't faze the crimson, and he retaliated in turn. Every blow jarred Groth, and blood flowed from his face.

Frafnar felt the impact of each strike as if they were his own. Visions of countless encounters with those who wanted to hurt him. They said he was weak. He didn't deserve to be there.

Stop, Frafnar thought.

Another strike to the jaw sent Groth reeling. The crimson followed up with a kick to Groth's midsection while he lay in the dirt.

A burden. Worthless. A useless twig.

Stop! Frafnar's slingshot was in his hand before he could blink. He plopped a rock in the pocket and let it soar. The stone flew wide of its target and rebounded off a tree. Maybe he needed more practice...

The crimson jerked his attention in the direction of the noise. Groth found his feet and charged the crimson, head bent and back arched. He rammed into the red-skinned brute and wrapped his arms around his stomach and squeezed with a roar. Groth tried to lift the suckling off his feet, but the crimson bobbed up briefly and was quick to slam his fists like hammers against Groth's back, who slumped to the ground. Frafnar had a new stone ready when two more pairs of feet passed by.

"You got him?" the first voiced asked, staring at Groth who panted on the ground.

"Where's the horn?" another asked, his red irises darting back and forth in the black of his eyes.

"Find it," said the one who'd fought Groth.

Smack.

Frafnar's stone hit the first orc's back, who looked behind him and glared at his companion, seeming to think it was him. The second glared right back before continuing to search the ground.

Smack!

The second whirled, rubbing his rump and getting in the face of the first. "You want a beating?"

The first pushed his face against the second's. "Do you?"

The two crimsons were getting violent when Frafnar spotted Groth's horn in front of him, a few feet beyond the foliage. Groth's expectant gaze settled on him before his eyelids fluttered closed. A movement from above froze Frafnar's whirling mind, and he instinctively spun behind the nearest tree. A crimson dropped onto the horn, the broken pieces grinding beneath his boots.

"Found it."

SUNDOWN

H e dead?" one of the crimsons asked.

"Still breathing, but we can fix that. He won't be warning anyone."

Frafnar's heart raced. What could he do?

"Wait. He'd be perfect for the pit. He's a quick one, even if he's old and can take a beating. I would've liked to fight him when he was strong."

"There'll be plenty to choose from soon."

"But most warriors die. We should keep him."

"Fine. You want him, you carry him."

"Heh. He's gonna get me so much grub."

Frafnar squeezed the slingshot. He couldn't keep track of who'd said what, but it didn't matter. They were crimsons, which meant everyone was in trouble. Groth wanted him to use the horn to warn Hammerstone, but it was in pieces. His father's horn dug into his back as he pressed himself against the base of the tree, reminding him of it. He slid it around to his chest. If he used it, the crimsons would know—

"What are you doing?"

A huge double-sided axe cut the air overhead and embedded itself in the wood. Frafnar slid lower, his mouth open but his throat constricted, and nothing came out as he trembled.

He bolted, putting all his fear into his strides.

"It's a runt!" a crimson hollered.

"The horn's crushed, he's good as dead."

Frafnar breathed again. They hadn't noticed his own horn.

"He's mine!"

Frafnar's heart jumped in his throat.

"The master will... Ah well. Your head, not mine."

Frafnar heard no more, and he didn't dare look back.

"The crimsons are coming."

"I know," Sera replied, "and that's why Frafnar should go to the Order if he can."

"I thought they would've found us out years ago. The sucklings must be getting lazy," Dejara said. "Finished your voodoo trap yet?"

"Are you even listening to me?"

Dejara sighed. "My brother's pigheaded, and you're just as stubborn as he. You've been having this argument for years."

"Now it's different. Frafnar has gritt. What if I can't

help him resist the demons?" Sera said, pacing the walkway above the main gate.

Dejara stood as firm as a rock and shrugged. "Orcs are used to hard roads."

"So, you agree with him then?"

"It doesn't matter what I think. It's between you two."

"He could come back if the Order doesn't accept him," Sera murmured. Her hopes were torn when she imagined Frafnar's future.

"Maybe once the sucklings make their move." Dejara tapped the end of her spear on the stone floor. "Is the voodoo done or not?"

"Hmm? Oh... yes. The gates are done, thanks mainly to the wisdom and aid of the mages this trade season."

The sun was beyond the horizon now, its light still lingering across the western horizon.

"It's time," Dejara called out. Moments later, the wood and metal portcullis dropped, and the wooden reinforcing doors banged shut.

"Open the gate!" an unexpected voice yelled from below.

"It can't be..." Sera said and joined Dejara at the edge of the wall.

Armastus approached on a cart beside an old human with a mule leading them.

Dejara slammed the side of her fist onto the stone parapet. "We just closed the damn thing!"

14

WARNING

The hard thumps of the crimson's footfalls drummed in Frafnar's ears above the pounding of his own heart. Terror tempted him to run straight and true, as far as he could, as fast as he could. But, because of Groth's drills, it was second nature to zigzag erratically through the trees.

"I'm not afraid. Orcs are not afraid." He clenched his teeth. The pep talk didn't help much.

After the third crossbow bolt zipped past his shoulders, he dug the side of his boot into the dirt and used the inertia to draw back on his loaded slingshot. The crimson charged forward, ignoring the runt's toy, and Frafnar fired.

A mix of desperation, luck, and an orc's arrogance allowed Frafnar's projectile to connect. The stone struck the crimson's throat causing him to choke, trip, and fall. Frafnar sped onward. It wouldn't be long until the crimson recovered, more peeved than ever.

The old watchtower he'd passed earlier came to Frafnar's frantic mind. It wasn't hard to find despite the darker shadows, and he scrambled up a rope that groaned in protest. He pulled himself into the watchtower, the wood so rotten he thought he might fall through. After catching his breath, he lifted the horn to his lips, then hesitated. If he'd succeeded in escaping the crimson, he would be giving himself away. His family was in danger… but they were safe behind thick walls and locked gates by now. What of his father? He could wait to see if—

A groan from the rope froze Frafnar in place.

"You're dead, runt," the crimson wheezed.

When the orc reached the top, Frafnar greeted him with a wide grin. While sitting, he used his feet to hold his slingshot's handle, one hand to keep the stone back and ready, his other hand holding the horn. Frafnar couldn't see the orc's shadowed face in detail, but the crimson would see his clear enough.

In a matter of seconds, the stone smacked the crimson in the face, the rope snapped, and Frafnar's deep breath flowed through the horn.

"Armastus, what are you doing here?" Sera greeted him as the cart creaked into Hammerstone.

The gate clunked shut behind them, and the doors were resealed, accompanied by a slew of cursing from Dejara. The gates were heavy and cumbersome, not meant to be opened and closed on a whim. Armastus jumped from his seat, ready to let others lead the troublesome human and his apples to safe quarters.

The old human raised his cane and poked the air repeatedly in Armastus's direction. "Where's everyone? The market's empty."

"I told you—" Armastus caught himself before his temper got the better of him. He ignored the senile old human and focused on his mate. *Horn,* he mouthed silently so she alone could see his empty hands.

Understanding lit Sera's eyes, and she changed her question. "What's he doing here?" she motioned to the newcomer.

"He's confused. Thought it was trading season."

"More apples for winter," a bold grayback cheered and tried to nab one.

Whack.

"Hands off the goods," the human warned with his cane. "Unless you have valuables to trade."

Sera was about to hand Armastus her horn when Erik came running. He panted heavily between his words. "Have you seen Fraf—? He said you forgot... horn... can't find him."

"You left without your horn?" a gray asked, overhearing.

"Did you check the side gates?" Concern creased Sera's face.

More grays joined in to poke fun at Armastus, who glared back at them. Their laughter died when one long horn call sounded in the distance, the dreaded signal they'd all been preparing for. Reality took a moment to sink in.

The crimsons had come.

15

ENCROACHING SHADOWS

"False alarm?" Erik proposed, voicing Sera's thoughts.

Everyone stood stock-still while they waited for confirmation. Colors of red and orange dominated the western horizon, reaching high above Hammerstone's walls as if the world was on fire. Were they ready if it proved true?

Another horn blared. Numerous more echoed from the western watchtowers, erasing any doubt. The inhabitants of Hammerstone burst into action like a frenzied beehive. Each had their part to play and all knew the drill. Warriors gathered to the walls while runts, protectors, and noncombatants swarmed to the Hole under the central tower.

"Watch out for Frafnar," Sera reminded her family before any of them moved.

Dejara acknowledged her with a two-fingered salute and grabbed Erik's arm. "You're with me," she said, dragging her husband to the north gate.

Sera shared a look with Armastus before he took off southward. He should've been on the main gate, but the magic she needed to channel was all linked here and someone had to organize the grays at the south gate. Here, the warriors kept their distance from the west entrance, per her orders. They'd learned long ago not to challenge the Pale Witch.

Sera fought the gnawing maternal instinct to jump the wall and search for Frafnar. She had to stay. Hammerstone would certainly be lost without her magic. She expected a Remnent would lead the charge, but if they got lucky, maybe a mere demose. Either way, she simply had to stay.

More watchtowers signaled their warnings, and Sera took her position above the gate. A gray stood ready near a horn as large as she was tall. This was it, the day they'd prepared for. The dawning of a world where grays stood tall against the crimsons. They'd come a long way since the first year settling here, expecting to be attacked for their rebellious plans. A time before walls and stone.

Now, ready or not, the crimsons had come. She dared dream that Hammerstone might one day withstand all that the crimsons and their masters could throw at it. Maybe they could get aid from the Order... But the truth crept in, and she shivered.

Please, let us endure more than one night at least, Sera prayed. She pressed her fingers on the cool surface of the parapet and stared out the opening. While she prepared for the coming trials, her worry for Frafnar's well-being deepened the heavy feeling inside her.

Frafnar wiped the moisture from his forehead. He threw the

leather strap of his horn over his shoulders and trembled with giddy elation from the aftershock, realizing what he'd achieved. Another signal horn mimicked his warning, shortly followed by more. He had to return to Hammerstone quickly. His father would—

The watchtower shook violently, jarring his thoughts. Frafnar peered down to find the crimson had recovered and was hacking away the supports with his axe. The old wood cracked under the crimson's might, and the tower tilted and groaned. Frafnar clung to a beam for dear life, trying not to cry out like a suckling when the watchtower crashed to the dirt. He tumbled out before the structure broke into a pile of splinters, mindful to jump away safely. He heard the crimson's axe destroy what remained of the structure as its wielder searched for him. He could get some distance between them, but soon the orc would realize he'd escaped.

Frafnar ran. The evening shadows that enveloped the world tripped him several times. He abandoned his zigzags for a straight course, new horn calls spurring him on. When the road cut through his path, he stumbled onto it, kicking up dust. Behind him, a frustrated roar resounded through the air. A horn blared in the trees across the way. The lookout would destroy the watchtower and retreat to Hammerstone after spying trouble.

Was that all the horns?

"Wait," Frafnar croaked. "Wait!"

16

CRIMSON WAVE

The watchtower was on fire when Frafnar passed by, the flames a guiding beacon. He rubbed his eyes, which were watering and stinging from the smoke. The tainted air invaded his lungs, and he shied away from the heat of the burning structure.

There was no sign of the lookout, who was probably scaling Hammerstone by now. Sure enough, when Frafnar reached the tree line, the gray was halfway up the wall, thanks to the defenders pulling the rope from above.

Plumes of glowing ash rose above the treetops where the other watchtowers stood. Crimsons chased the lookouts, firing crossbows. Frafnar spun around when the watchtower collapsed behind him into a burning heap. Across the flames stood his crimson pursuer, the fury in his red eyes promising death.

Frafnar dashed for the wall, sounding off a sharp whistle. The lookout's ascent slowed, and a head popped into view from above the wall.

"Fraf!" Dejara called. "Hurry!"

He ran, jumping over tree stumps and kicking loose rocks. An exposed rock, well camouflaged with caked dry mud, caught the tip of his boot, which sent him sprawling. A thick rope snaked down and hit the dirt with a thud. Frafnar scrambled through the soil and rolled over a layer of straw and took hold of the loop on the end. It pulled him to his feet. He climbed it and secured a foot in the loop.

Frafnar was only a few feet in the air when the crimson roared from the edge of the forest. More crimsons emerged from deeper shadows under the trees, swarming the north wall and gate. Their numbers grew, spreading southward toward Frafnar.

"Fire!" Dejara yelled.

Torches dropped from atop the gate onto the straw and oil that skirted the outside wall. A chorus of screams joined the inferno as the fire spread along the treeless yard, engulfing all in its path. The light of it grew brighter as it headed for Frafnar.

"Heave," Dejara commanded those on the rope.

Frafnar was only a fraction of the lookout's weight so he rose quickly, but a clang of metal against stone made him flinch. The axe fell harmlessly, and an orc roared above the others. Undeterred by the approaching inferno, the crimson leaped at his prey. The orc caught Frafnar's ankle and latched on.

The added weight dragged the rope down a few feet before it caught and rose again, the ascent slowing considerably. Frafnar kicked and jerked, but the crimson held firm. The fire swept across the ground below them, the rising heat hot on the soles of their boots.

Frafnar's attempts to remove his extra baggage failed. The crimson climbed him, and when he had a firm hold on the rope, he retrieved an item from the back of his belt. Light from the flames gleamed off sharp steel. Frafnar flailed in a last desperate attempt, but the orc raised his dagger for the strike.

Blood sprayed Frafnar when a spear tore into the space between the crimson's neck and shoulder. The orc lost his hold on the rope, and his cries rang out as the flames consumed him.

From above, Dejara disappeared back out of sight. "Get him up."

When Frafnar reached the top, Dejara and Erik helped him over the ledge. They all collapsed, panting hard, except for his aunt who playfully punched his shoulder.

"Glad you could make it."

17

ENEMY AT THE GATE

Master Valrix rubbed the drying blood between her fingers. Her anger was momentarily sated by killing the nearest orc—fortunate for the prime who was away relaying orders—when the horn warned Hammerstone of their approach. The high from the kill was already fading, but the rhythm of marching boots helped soothe her urges. After all, the night had just begun.

A crescendo of weapons banging against shields and metal rose above all else as Valrix led her army south toward Hammerstone. Abandoned watchtowers crumbled in fiery blazes beside the road—to Valrix, the perfect sight to welcome them.

The prime's rigid strides didn't go unnoticed as he guarded her flank. Valrix would have openly shared her amusement at his unease if she hadn't been busy enjoying the precursors of battle.

The last bend in the path brought Hammerstone into view, the gate secured, wild flames raging along the left side of its walls. The crimson army halted shy of the tree line. The entrance only remained clear of fire by the cobblestone ground. The light revealed shadows on the battlements. An unmarked human face stood out amid the grays.

There was no need for words, no chance to surrender. Those of Hammerstone knew their crimes and their consequences. The crimson crescendo halted, and in one fluid motion Valrix let loose an arrow from her bow, the magic-infused missile arcing through the air above the wall. The barrier surrounding Hammerstone appeared in a flash of light and deflected the deadly skewer. Ripples spread from the spot then faded, like a pebble plopping into a still pond. The human woman's face lifted in satisfaction at the small victory.

Valrix pointed and crimsons fired bolts, pelting the gate. Small sacks of oil attached to the projectiles bounced against the wooden portcullis, some bursting and drenching their mark with black sludge. A final bolt, alight with fire, ignited the gate in a burst of flame. The light reflected in the eyes of the crimson warriors as they cheered. Bags of mud dropped from the wall, but the next volley of crimson bolts slowed their work.

The fire to the left of the wall continued to burn, and the flames danced suggestively. Valrix wouldn't deny them, and the thought of using the defenses against the grays made it a deliciously easy decision.

Redirecting the inferno was simple for Valrix. A tendril of fire arched up and assaulted the gate. Hammerstone's magical barrier was useless against ordinary elemental fire, and the heat did its job to weaken the barricade.

When the inferno was depleted, the portcullis remained

intact but was visibly permeable. It just needed one last push. The bulk of crimson warriors parted to let her weapon pass. Valrix soaked in the nervous stares from the defenders above. A large glowing rune slid along the ground, rotating as it moved, the boulder within it rolling along inside. With a wave of her arm, the rock flew and a barrage of crimson bolts joined it.

Valrix grinned like a cat on the hunt. She did so enjoy when her prey chose to put up a fight.

18

BREACH

Cover!" Sera warned, raising her shield above her head. Some grays scrambled inside the battlement corridors while others out in the open squeezed together to create a horizontal shield wall. The ground shook from the impact of the boulder, forcing those in Sera's company to cling to one another. A crash below, followed by wet smacks and silenced cries, was enough to know the gate was breached.

Crimsons broke formation and charged the opening. Defenders took down some and wounded others through slits in the stone, but the crimsons pushed on. Inside, the grays left distance between themselves and the gate, formations of sturdy warriors engaging the crimsons who survived.

"Signal the horns," Sera commanded.

A gray took a deep breath behind her, and the resonating horn blast filled the air. Three others joined it from far along the battlements. Sera handed her shield to the gray beside her, who kept it in place over them while she closed her eyes and concentrated on the sound. She welcomed the notes into her, weaving a spell. The mages had been meticulous about the workings of the magic, and she followed their instructions exactly.

Sera didn't need to see the rune that appeared at her feet to know it was there, glowing brighter as the power built. She trembled from the mental strain that threatened to tear her apart, but she waited. Time slowed in her mind's eye, and the noise of battle felt far away. She held out a hand, palm down, and wrapped the other around her wrist. The energy of the magic flowed out of the rune like a burst faucet, holding the barrier around Hammerstone. Compressing the power proved more challenging than releasing it.

The grays around her stood their ground like ancient trees in a storm, unaffected by the raging gusts of air. All Sera saw were stoic figures with set jaws and light reflecting in their eyes. She dropped to a knee and pushed until her hand touched the rune. Sound came rushing back to her, the howling wind above all else. A couple thumps from more bolts hit the shields before the ground rumbled anew. The grays knelt with her for better balance, and more cries of death were lost amid the scraping of stone.

When the tremors subsided, Sera rose to view the city. Fresh walls had sprung up, creating a maze of narrow passages inside the three gates. The advance of crimsons had decreased considerably, but when Sera viewed the battle below, more crimsons than she'd expected fought beyond her new defenses. *The spell took too long*, she thought and chewed her lip.

"Reinforce the breached areas," Sera ordered, and the

grays departed. She reclaimed her shield but was not ready for it, and took a moment to rest. A group of grays scattered to fortify the slits in her conjured walls, preventing the outside enemy from joining the horde already inside.

Sera breathed in the crisp evening air that partially restored her drained energy from the spellcasting. The grays were starting to prevail over the crimson forces within their home when a burning mass arced across the sky, a plume of smoke behind it.

Indeed, the barrier no longer encompassed all of Hammerstone.

19

WITHIN CHAOS

Bromh witnessed the new barrier surround the central tower. The magic appeared as little more than a thin sphere of golden light, and he felt nothing when he crossed it. Was this really their last defense?

The inhabitants of Hammerstone herded to the Hole and the tunnel beneath. Bromh moved with them, scanning the crowd. The going was slow, if only they'd been warned sooner. They needed more time. He turned against the flow, but a heavy hand landed on the back of his neck.

"Wrong way, runt," a defender growled at him.

A momentary glance at his brothers signaled them to start shoving and barking overacted insults at one another. The distraction successful, Bromh slipped from the protector and took a more diagonal approach. Soon he escaped into the shadows of the buildings and headed for the main gate. Everyone would celebrate when he killed all the crimsons and they wouldn't have to leave—

A fireball cut the sky, interrupting his thoughts and

demolishing the building next to him. The boulder crashed through the structure, ricocheting off the insides and out a window. The rolling mass of death narrowly missed him. The building groaned as the walls toppled and smoking rubble spewed out with it, right atop Bromh who leaped for cover.

"Time to go," Dejara said, guiding Frafnar and Erik down through the passages of the wall.

Frafnar got in the way of the many grays who brushed past them. Erik caught his arm and positioned him behind Dejara so that the trio descended the steps in single file. The next tremor slowed their progress, everyone grasping wildly for an anchor. The shaking lasted longer this time, dust and loose pebbles falling from the ceiling.

When the quakes stopped, Dejara directed them to follow, leaping a handful of steps at a time in her race to the bottom. His aunt was already outside by the time Frafnar caught up.

"She did it." Dejara marveled at the newly constructed defenses at her gate.

Erik joined them next, huffing. "Need... more... cardio."

The thud of bolts landing nearby and fire streaking above snapped Dejara out of her trance. She retrieved a spear from a weapons rack, shoved a small wooden shield into Erik's hands, and tossed Frafnar a buckler. Frafnar's excitement grew while his uncle frowned.

"Sera wanted us to take her son to the Hole," Erik said,

struggling to keep up with Dejara as she headed for the west gate. He tugged on her forearm to slow her.

Other grays rushed by as Dejara shot an annoyed look at her mate. "She said to keep an eye out. He's found, now he can fight." She pulled her arm free.

Erik's mouth was partway open when Frafnar distracted him. "No time for a debate, they need us at the breach."

The man paled a shade, considering the rock and the hard place he was wedged between. Sera or Dejara: whose ire did he fear more?

"I could get you there myself and come back," Erik answered diplomatically, appearing to have found a compromise.

Frafnar slapped an arm around his uncle and squeezed. "There'll be wounded," he said while admiring his not-so-shiny buckler. "They can't wait."

Clarity twinkled in Erik's eyes, and he straightened. "You're right." He sighed. "But, be careful or Sera will—"

If Erik said more, the words were lost in the loud crash when a fiery boulder smashed through a building like a wrecking ball. Stunned, the pair stared at the smoking carnage. Frafnar led Erik after Dejara before the man could lose his resolve.

20

DEFENSIVE LINE

Dejara was already barking orders and organizing the grays beyond the first defensive line when Frafnar and Erik arrived. Carts, barrels, crates, even the trade stands were stacked in a line that enclosed the area to the gate and the magically raised walls. Heat radiated from the defensive line as fire burned the wood in the hastily piled barrier, deterring the crimsons from trying to scale it. The only way through was a gap, a straight shot from the gate.

"Frafnar, get up there and help ready the second line." Dejara pointed to the nearest roof before turning her attention back to the defensive line.

Erik needed no instructions; he was already yanking a bolt from a gray's buttocks, who instantly charged into the fray again.

Frafnar shot a stone from his sling through the gap, missing the head he'd been aiming for, but into the eye of another. Lucky it hadn't been a gray. The crimson he'd missed sank a wicked blade into the midsection of a gray, the tip of the weapon emerging out his back, blood dripping from it. With a curl of his lip, the crimson lifted a foot and freed his victim from the blade.

Frafnar took a step back, his spirit shaken. The smell of smoke couldn't mask the stench of death. The grays remobilized from the crimson rush, and the tight formation of graybacks blocked Frafnar's view. Dejara screamed at him to go pull the lever atop the building, and only then did his legs comply.

He scrambled up the nearest ladder. The grays responsible for preparing the second defense worked their way from the structures near the outer wall inward to further pen the crimsons in and gradually decrease the gap through which the grays could escape.

The heap of wood, boulders, scrap metal, and other rubbish was easy to spot; it was the hail of flaming boulders that gave Frafnar pause. Dwellings toppled; smoke and glowing embers filled the air while fires raged.

Frafnar sprang to the lever to release the mound destined to block the street below. It wasn't about to move readily because of the load it held, and he grunted from trying. Victory was his when he leaped on the thing with his full weight. The debris tumbled down, but Frafnar's whoop of triumph was cut short when one of the enemy boulders smashed through his building.

The roof shook, and Frafnar held on to the lever, expecting the structure to crumble beneath his feet. The builders could've been proud of their work, for they'd constructed the sturdiest frame. But how were they to know a boulder the size of a bull would be slammed through it?

The building tipped, and Frafnar with it.

21

LITTLE VICTORIES

Frafnar bent his knees and jumped as far as he could. The roof tilted at a steep angle, so he used the momentum to propel himself forward. He sprang through the air, his entire body outstretched beyond comfort.

A drying line passed the length of his fingers and right into his palms. Frafnar tightened his grip around the lifeline and swung safely above the mishmash below. "Yes!" he whooped, but the drying rope failed to hold at one end.

"No—" His smile dropped as fast as he did.

The prime tossed aside the corpse, the shield he'd used to make it through the corridors of death inside Hammerstone's gate. Other crimsons mimicked his technique to maneuver past the grayback spears that stabbed at them from slits in the walls.

The ground was littered with numerous crimson bodies,

but those who survived focused on killing the grays behind the spears first. Regardless, their numbers still entered Hammerstone at a dismal rate.

The prime and a few other orcs escaped to the corner between the wall and the flaming barricade. The warriors held off any grays that came too close while the prime considered the barrier. When there was a break in the gray resistance, the prime commanded those with him to use their shields and push the blazing cart. Stacks of wood, stone, and pieces of sharp metal were piled atop and beneath it, but the crimsons were able to move the cart with their combined strength.

Once they broke through, the warriors surged to attack the grays from behind. The prime studied the next barrier as more crimsons poured through the gap. A larger mound of scrap blocked the way between buildings. On a whim, the prime looked for a way past, all the way to the wall. Lo and behold, the debris didn't quite fill all the way to the stone. He just might be able to squeeze through.

22

ALIVE AND BURIED

Vibrations coaxed Bromh awake to feel his face pressed against cool stone. Pebbles cascaded down between larger chunks of rock and wood, pelting him like hail. He coughed, feeling like all the dust in the world had gathered in his lungs. What started as a dull headache became sharp pain.

Disorientated, Bromh crawled forward, acting on impulse. He swept the debris aside until he could go no farther. The distance was only a couple feet, but it felt like yards. Between the gaps in the wreckage that blocked his path, the sight of freedom taunted him.

He rubbed dust from his eyes and propped himself up into a sitting position. With his back to the way out, he pushed with his legs, hoping to break free. Instead, the rubble shifted, causing more to fall and make his prison more confined.

The chill of fear pulled his mind back into focus, and he curled up to become a smaller target while his tomb

punished him for trying to escape. When the shifting stopped, the bruise on his shoulder complained the most. He pushed the new debris away and peered through the gaps once more.

Bromh clenched his teeth. No one was visible, and the surge of pride and panic competed for control. Orcs don't need help. But he was only a runt. Orcs don't cry out. But what was he to do? He took a shaky deep breath, trying not to choke on dust. He could do this; he had to find a way.

The ground shook again, and the stone fell and found his foot this time. He yelped and kicked the rock with the heel of his other foot. If he didn't hurry, this place would become his actual tomb.

Shadows moved beyond the gaps, and Bromh's panic won the battle. Someone was there! His whistle pierced the air while shame melted his insides.

Frafnar wandered the streets searching for a way around toppled buildings and burning rubble. There had to be a street that led back to the defensive line. He rubbed his side, sore from slamming into a building while dangling from the rope. It could've been worse, so when he heard a sharp whistle he was eager to investigate.

The sound drew him to an inconspicuous pile of debris, a sight now unsettlingly common in Hammerstone. He answered in kind, trying to find the source in the shadows.

There was no response.

Frafnar whistled again and kept still, waiting, listening.

Nothing cut through the noise of distant battle, crumbling buildings, and explosions. Had he imagined it?

A flaming boulder crashed into the street down the way. The ground trembled and stone shifted.

"Here! Here—I'm here!" a desperate voice called out.

Frafnar's attention swung from the blazing mass to a mound of rubble. As he carefully inspected the heap of stone, a hand sprang at him from a dark hole.

"I'm trapped."

Dreams of being a hero played in Frafnar's mind. "I'll get you out."

"You?" the voice scoffed. "No, get someone else."

"I can do it."

"Don't touch it! Move the wrong thing and it'll all come down."

Frafnar froze.

"Typical twig. Can't even do something simple."

Annoyance struck Frafnar like a punch, instantly connecting the voice and insults to a certain nasty runt. Frafnar stomped off, shaking. He could leave; after all, Bromh deserved no less for all the torment he had caused. If he died, no one would know... but only a real twig would do that.

"Good," Bromh said. "You're useless anyway."

A slight quiver tainted the angry words. A part of Frafnar relished Bromh's panic while another part berated himself for it. He wanted to rage at the world for putting him in this position on the worst day imaginable, but instead he comforted himself with a compromise. He marched back.

"Admit you need my help!" he yelled.

"You couldn't help a horse find grass," Bromh answered stubbornly.

"Well, there's no one else." Frafnar eyed a broken plank among some wreckage, close to where Bromh was buried. It took some effort to pull it free from the heavy stone, but he managed. The noise of shifting rubble clearly put Bromh on edge. "No, you'll get me killed! Or—maybe that's what you're hoping for..."

"Don't be an idiot," Frafnar said while carefully testing a few of the stones around Bromh. "I'd rather see the look on your face when I'm the one who saves you."

"I'm dead. You can't do anything... unless you use that voodoo. Use it to lift all the—"

Wood clunked against stone as Frafnar wedged the plank into a gap.

"All I need is a little leverage."

23

FRIENDLY FIRE

As the flow of crimsons entering the gate slowed, Valrix increased the frequency and intensity of her assaults. A second portal opened, and she conjured another large rune beneath it. Now, with two pathways to shuttle the boulders across, she seemed to have an endless supply of ammunition. Crimsons lathered the stones with pitch and set them ablaze before transporting them through the other end of the portals. Twin piles of flaming boulders flanked Valrix.

The Pale Witch could barely keep up to the hail of stone, deflecting what she could. White runes appeared in the path of the fiery streaks, knocking them aside and raining death upon the crimsons outside.

Valrix shot a slab directly at Sera, who disappeared, and the lip of the wall broke from the impact. Certain the woman still lived, Valrix laughed. "Is it familiar? I hope you appreciate the irony of being beaten with the spoils from your allies." She flexed her fingers and telekinetically flung five stones from each of her piles.

"Tonight, Hammerstone falls."

The prime sank his blade deep into the gray orc. He'd made no attempt to conceal himself, but the gray had been preoccupied with trying to put out fires. A sack slipped from the gray's hands, and mud splattered the cobblestone. The gray fell into the muck, staining it a deep red.

Now behind the defensive lines, the prime freely roamed the settlement. He avoided groups and picked off the lone orcs. The unmarred buildings he explored appeared empty, so he stuck to the streets, which too had few grays traveling them. They couldn't all be fighting, could they? At least the runts had to be hidden somewhere. The sky lit up as more streaks of fire pummeled Hammerstone. If only he could find the runts, he'd force the grays to submit. Pathetic. More slaves to bear the burden for his people.

Around the next bend, the prime was rewarded with a stroke of luck. A runt struggled to move debris. An arm emerged from the mound, but the rest of the body was still trapped.

The prime squeezed the hilt of his sword and leaped into a run. These creatures weren't orcs. He roared, hoping the little scamp would flee like the vermin it was. He was so fixated on his quarry that when the building to his right exploded, he looked up too late.

"Mast—?"

24

CRUMBLE

What was that?" Bromh asked, trying to see where the noise came from.

The surrounding area brightened. Frafnar heard the roar and the collapse of a nearby building. He'd been busy wedging aside a stone, so all he saw was the aftermath over his shoulder.

"No idea," he answered, his attention focused on the rescue. With enough leverage, he used the plank to shift the stone. This made it the best chance to get Bromh out. Gradually, it moved far enough that Bromh could squeeze his shoulders into the gap. Frafnar pulled him until both he and Bromh fell back and the other runt was finally free.

The ground quaked as a massive explosion rocked Hammerstone, and the pile of rubble completely collapsed. Bromh stared at it, realizing how close death had come, and Frafnar flashed him his biggest smile.

"You're welcome."

A dozen more projectiles arced toward Hammerstone, and Sera knelt beside the damaged wall, trying to catch her breath. Fortified with the strength of a demon, the woman was relentless. The little energy Sera had left was fueling the magic field around the Hole.

As she took a moment to rest—while trying not to think about the deaths wrought by the boulders she failed to stop —Sera eyed the slab of stone. *Spoils from your allies.* The weight of the words hit home. The other settlements were lost, and the rubble was being used as ammunition to...

Like a waking volcano, the rage spread through her, building until her hands shook. They had worked endlessly to better the lives of the grays. They'd known the crimsons would interfere one day, but the woman's cruel disposition twisted the proverbial knife. It was too much.

Sera found energy in her anger and used it. All the weapons waiting on their racks vibrated and flew into the air, straight at the demose. "Our lives are not for you to toy with like we're nothing," she declared. If anyone had a chance to repel the crimsons for a time, it was Hammerstone.

The demose protected herself with the slabs of stone. "You *are* nothing," she answered, launching more of the debris from the fallen settlements.

Adrenaline and emotion fueled Sera as she continued to divert the boulders. She dared a peek over her shoulder, and her chest ached at the sight of the burning buildings. She turned back in time to block the next boulder aimed at her head, but a piece of the slab broke off and clipped her above the ear. The rest of the boulder deflected at a bad angle and crashed into the top of the wall several dozen paces away. A great crack split the stone.

The attacks ceased while the demose analyzed the fracture. Her grin spread wide, and she threw everything she had at the weakened area. The three biggest boulders hit their mark, one above the other. One. Two. Three. And that section of the wall ripped open like a gaping wound.

25

DEBT

Bromh shoved Frafnar. "I didn't ask for your help, twig."

The words sounded familiar, and a memory played in Frafnar's mind when he replied. "You didn't have to."

A horn call interrupted Bromh's next quip. The following silence was deafening, and the bombardment of flying boulders ceased. Unsure what was happening, Frafnar eyed Bromh's limp. "Maybe I should get you to the Hole. Would be a shame if saving you turned out to be pointless."

"Shut it. If you tell anyone, I'll kill you."

"Oh, I'm trembling in my boots."

Bromh flinched like he'd been stabbed in the back and grabbed the front of Frafnar's jerkin. The runt's face was inches from his, but Frafnar refused to yield, staring back defiantly. He wasn't the one who felt ashamed. Bromh wasn't stupid. He clearly knew this, and he shoved Frafnar again before hobbling away. "I'll get even," he said. "I won't owe anything to a twig."

They searched for a way to the defensive line, and as time went on Bromh's limp improved. The clang of metal alerted them before they reached the next street. Grays slowly retreated north while engaging the crimsons. Dejara and Erik were among them. Frafnar's aunt enacted an impressive shield-spear combo that penetrated a crimson's defenses.

Bromh stared with a stupid look of admiration. "Dejara's amazing..."

Frafnar almost gagged, unable to take Bromh ogling his aunt. *It better not be a crush,* he thought. *That'd be—* His stomach churned. Frafnar used his sling and volleyed rocks to busy his mind.

A crimson was quick to decide that two runts were easy targets and bounded toward them. A rock to the head didn't deter him, and Frafnar fell back when the orc's blade swung, sliding harmlessly across his buckler but slicing the band of his sling. Bromh was large for a runt, and he used this advantage to close the distance to the crimson and elbow the wind out of him. Dejara arrived in time to finish the job.

Frafnar somberly discarded his broken sling when Dejara spoke.

"The wall's breached, we're falling back." She tapped Frafnar's shoulder with the back of her shield before reimmersing herself in the fight.

Frafnar continued to pelt the horde of crimsons with rocks, but the strength of his arm was unequal to the sling. When a gray tossed a thick rope at Bromh to use, the runt looked at it in disbelief, clearly expecting a real weapon. He stooped for the dead crimson's blade, but another orc rushed him before he could retrieve it. A fistful of rocks in the crimson's eyes gave Bromh time to leap away.

"Get back," Dejara screamed at them, and grays edged between the runts and the invading forces.

"You're welcome... again." Frafnar beamed.

Bromh clenched his teeth and wrung the rope like it was Frafnar's neck.

26

MORE TROUBLE

Crimsons surged into Hammerstone's new breach like water down an open drain. Valrix's strut was slow, and she deliberately overdramatized her movements. She held her chin high and her hands up and spread out, absorbing the destruction. Bodies lay strewn across the ground among the rubble, and any wounded gray survivors were cut down.

A horn sounded from the wall with a haunting tone. Valrix found it suitable as she headed for the falling star drifting down from the sky. When she'd placed it above the barrier that had surrounded Hammerstone, she'd aimed it above the central tower, but the star had slid off course. No matter, it wasn't needed now, so why waste it? Valrix quickened her pace to collect it before it touched down.

The deeper she and her troops delved into Hammerstone, the more grays they encountered. Maybe the horn was a rallying call rather than one of retreat?

By this time, the number of crimsons around her dwindled as they spread through Hammerstone, and the few that remained with her battled an increasing number of grays. It wasn't until she passed between buildings, and felt the change in the air as the passage closed behind them, that she realized their plan. An ambush!

Sera dropped the horn from her lips after the single note. It had to be enough. The world spun, and for a time, it was all she could do to sit up. She heard the crimsons violating her home. "It's not over yet," she vowed.

After a time, the world righted itself and she carefully stood. Many of the zip lines that connected the top of the wall to areas in Hammerstone were severed, snapped because of the boulders or toppled buildings. A few remained intact, so Sera strapped her shield to her back and chose the rope that would land her closest to the head of the invading forces.

Crisp night air blew against her cheeks and whipped past her ears as she zipped above Hammerstone. Pockets of warmth rose from the fires below, and Sera held her breath through the billowing smoke.

From her vantage point, the movement of the crimsons was clear enough. The grays at the main gate had pulled back to the third defensive line, creating walls that would direct the crimsons toward the east side, giving the grays time to withdraw. The architects had done their jobs well. No matter which gate—or wall—was breached, the labyrinth-like layout made it troublesome for the invaders to reach the central tower. The tower itself was of little importance. What lay beneath was the only reason she'd agreed to this rebellion. Without means of escape, who would survive to defy the crimsons and their masters? As much as this was her home, it had been temporary from the start. Only with time had Hammerstone become what it was.

Then Sera saw it, and her breath caught in her throat. Above the settlement, a small winking light drifted down like a falling star. "Oh... no."

27

LIKE MOTHS TO A FLAME

The noise of Sera's descent drew the attention of a few crimsons. She tucked in her knees and curled her body until her heels faced the sky. Bolts flew, only one thudded against her shield, so they were obviously not versed in flying targets.

Sera righted herself once she zoomed over the second defensive line. *What are they doing?* she wondered, when the grays swarmed to the falling light. "I called for the retreat!" Orc stubbornness knew no bounds.

The zip line bounced her for an instant, and the surprise set her nerves on end. Through a plume of smoke, she located the section that had caught fire. *Hold, hold,* she thought. *Hold on.*

Below, crimsons searched buildings and scoured the streets. Not as great in number as the horde that streamed in from the broken wall, but even one crimson was troublesome enough. Would they find her corpse splattered on the cobblestones?

The second strand of rope burned apart. She was almost to the ground, she could make—

The final strand gave way, and she plummeted.

"Now!" Armastus signaled with a torch.

The gap closed on the heels of the demose who crossed it. The main crimson forces pushed south to get around, but a fair number had swarmed in before it closed. The crimsons charged ahead of their master, who seemed transfixed on a small light in the sky.

The grays had the advantage in numbers, bolstered by Armastus and his forces. The thunderous breach in the wall pressured them to abandon their posts and quickly set up new defenses, as well as this trap.

The grays intercepted the crimsons while the demose ignored them, her focus only on the light. She stopped beneath it, waiting. Armastus and a handful of other grays prevented crimson stragglers from trespassing into the heart of Hammerstone. Most grays converged on the lone woman, who concentrated on them only when they approached. She flashed a twisted grin. Her display of malice gave many of the stoutest warriors pause.

"Shall we dance?"

28

FALLING STAR

Falling, Sera squeezed her eyes shut, waiting for the agony, but it never came. A cool, feather-like kiss touched her cheek, encouraging an eye to open; snow drifted down among the ash as if winter had come early. Moving her arms disturbed the fluffy snow that half-buried her, lifting a thin cloud of ice pellets.

Flailing like a fish, it took some time for her to escape the snowbank she'd instinctively conjured. Soon, however, her boots touched cobblestone, and she blew into her cupped hands.

Sera sighed. How humiliating it would've been if she'd died from a mere fall, during a siege no less. She imagined the reports. The Pale Witch, slain by gravity. Well, not today! There were so many ways she could go tonight, and *that* would not be one of them. She was still here and relatively unharmed. Having wasted enough time, she pinpointed the falling star and continued onward. Time ticked away in the back of her mind, tightening the knot in her gut.

The star was the work of the demose, no doubt. The purpose of the barrier around Hammerstone was to deflect such an attack. But it was now only protecting the tower...

A few crimsons hollered at her from a path between buildings. Sera lifted her hand without pause, and a wall of ice rose to block them. Her shield thumped against her back when she ran, as if prodding her to pick up the pace. The clang of weapons and the roars of battle grew louder the closer she got.

"Retreat!" she yelled when she arrived. The training ground was clear of buildings, so she had a perfect view of the tight formation of grays that gathered beneath the falling star. Periodically a warrior was thrown back over the heads of the others. One such gray picked himself up a few feet from her, favoring his ribs while blood dripped from his lips.

Sera opened her mouth, but it was the voice of Armastus that filled the air.

"Pull back," he ordered from the defensive line.

"It's too late," she whispered, her body feeling heavy.

The injured gray must have heard her because he glanced from her to the falling star, which rested in the outstretched palm of the vile woman.

Sera watched helplessly as light seared the darkness, and all that stood within it.

29

INTO THE FRAY

"Eema!" Frafnar yelled as a light flashed like the sun itself. The explosion rocked the ground, staggering grays and crimsons alike. Even the crimsons paused at the sight of it, shielding their eyes.

Frafnar began to step forward when a hand clamped around his arm.

"You an idiot?" Bromh's hold tightened.

"Don't pretend to care." Frafnar tried to yank himself free. "Let go."

The fighting resumed, the grays being slowly pushed back to the final barrier surrounding the tower and the Hole beneath it. Wounded grays started trickling in from the direction of the blast.

Bromh snorted. "I *don't* care. Go get killed then," he said, releasing his grip and causing Frafnar to stumble. "Just one thing I owe you before you die." Frafnar did not expect the fist that swung at him, and the loud smack when it connected with his upper arm. "Don't let the crimsons snap you, twig," Bromh added, before returning to the fight.

"Sure," Frafnar managed in a high-pitched voice. *Ow*, he mouthed, turning away.

The arcane shield winked out of existence, and all Sera could do was raise her arms around her head as rubble rained on them. The injured gray grunted between breaths as heavy as Sera's. Despite his condition, he'd managed to haul them behind some cover moments before the blast, and her magic shield had anchored them.

"Take it."

Perplexed by the gray's sudden words, Sera found him offering his hand. He must have seen the confusion she felt.

"Take it," he repeated more forcefully. "Only you can stop the demon now."

"You'll need it—"

"You're weak." Anger rose in his voice, and he smashed the dirt. "Take it!"

She clasped his hand, and he calmed. She saw only steadfast resolve with abounding stubbornness gleaming in his eyes. Pulling the energy from him was like sucking a partially blocked straw. Slowly, but surely, it flowed into her.

After a time, she let go, and he slumped. She reached for his hand but he raised his palms outward and stood on his own.

"Get to the Hole," she said.

"Why did we name it that?" the gray grumbled, lumbering in that direction.

Sera watched after him until she heard the demose calling.

"Did anyone survive? I truly hope I didn't spoil the fun."

"Eema!" Frafnar hollered, then coughed. The smoke was thick, and he could only see a few paces ahead. Rubble crunched beneath his boots, and he navigated his way around larger blocks. Fires littered the destruction, the light giving the haze a red-orange glow.

Frafnar yelled for his mother again. There was no sign of any crimsons, the area eerily quiet except for distant indistinguishable sounds.

Panic tightened his insides the longer he searched. What if he couldn't find her? What if she was dead?

"E—" he began, but a flare of light caught his attention.

The sound of rapidly approaching footsteps was all he could hear. A hand took hold and pulled him as a light streaked past and scorched the ground behind them. Crouching behind a broken stone wall, Frafnar was about to speak when his mother put a finger to her lips.

"Go," she whispered. "Before..."

"Enough of this hide and seek!" another woman's voice shouted.

A wind picked up speed, flowing outward from the center. The haze cleared, and Frafnar could breathe deep again.

"Now," the woman continued. "Where were we?"

30

THE PALE WITCH

A hail of stone rained down and knocked against Sera's shield after each arcane assault. The ruined wall they used for cover was chipping away bit by bit from the impacts. Frafnar stayed close beside her but didn't cling.

"I know you hear the whispers," the demose called. "Why do you spurn them? Are you afraid you'll hurt your precious family?"

Of course, the demose felt the residual taint. Sera sensed Frafnar focus on her, but she couldn't meet his eyes. There was so much that he didn't know. She took a deep breath and flashed him a reassuring smile and mouthed, *Don't worry*.

"Hiding only prolongs the inevitable." Missile after missile of the woman's dark energy slammed into the base of the wall with such force that it cracked. "What will you do?"

She's right, Sera thought. *We can't last forever.*

"How do we beat her?"

Frafnar's question rose above the noise of the explosions.

Anger raged in his eyes, and Sera thought he might react impulsively and face the demose alone if there was a break in the assaults. He was so like his father it was uncanny. It gave her pause; he was orc after all.

The thought of Armastus tore at her heart. He might be gone. The devastation around them would become like a massive grave marker for all who lost their lives here, in the name of freedom.

Their situation revealed the truth to her. There'd be no escape for any of them, not if the demose still lived.

Sera straightened and raised her chin. Frafnar saw the spark of determination in her again.

"Stay here," she said, sweeping her arm out and closing her fist. A conjured blizzard enveloped the demose, allowing them a moment's reprieve.

Sera stepped into the currents of air created by the howling blizzard. Her silhouette was dark against the blue glow of the magic, her shield held ready by her side. In three strides Frafnar caught up. He touched her hand, and a swell of fear strained her features when she looked back.

Frafnar squeezed her hand. "I'm with you." He wouldn't back down.

Magic isn't a weakness. She'd been trying to make him understand, make him see and embrace who he was, so how could she deny him now?

Sera's expression softened. The unease remained, but she nodded.

"Together then."

31

TRUE GRITT

A blast of hot air burst outward from the demose, canceling the blizzard. "What's the plan?" Frafnar asked, turning with his mother toward their rival.

"Use her power against her."

The demose dusted the snow off her arms as if neutralizing the spell was a trivial matter. "You should know, you've been far too much trouble to be allowed to live." She rubbed her chin. "Although, torture is tempting..."

Frafnar erected a barrier around him and his mother, magic shimmering. The demose got the hint; the fight wasn't over. "So be it," she mused, readying her bow. Dark magic in the shape of an arrow formed in her hand.

"Fortunate for us your masters didn't think it important enough to send a Remnent, demon. If your host weren't merely a sorcerer, you'd have this day," Sera declared.

The woman's red eyes glowed, and her mouth parted in a snarl. She let loose on the taut bowstring, and the magic bolt launched.

Frafnar braced for the impact, but Sera, on the other hand, stood calmly. He sensed her power, her will that could snuff out magic or manipulate it.

Before the arcane missile rammed his shield, it froze in midair. The woman's face creased with a frown. "This cannot be."

The missile turned, painstakingly slow. The demose reached out, fingers clawing to wrestle for control. Sera gained mastery over it and sent the arcane arrow back to its maker.

A barrier was conjured in time to stop it. "Your command of gritt is pitiful," the demose spat. "Let's find your limit, shall we?"

Missile after missile shot from the woman's bow. A dozen projectiles converged on Frafnar's shield. Would it hold against them all?

Sweat stained Sera's blouse, the fabric clinging to her between leather armor as her free hand swept back and forth through the air. She took hold of the magic shots, colliding some, and repelling or eliminating others. Her will slipped from the last one, unable to stop it from slamming into their shield.

A force hit Frafnar's chest as solid as a fist. He staggered back, but his magic held. *And that had been only one?* Frafnar thought, taking a moment to catch his breath.

"Final volley," the demose jeered. "Enjoy your last moments." She released one arrow this time, which multiplied into twenty en route to its target.

Sera searched frantically for any cover they could use. Her chest heaved with each breath. She couldn't stop them all.

Frafnar heard the whispers, but the flicker of red in his mother's eyes betrayed what she'd sacrifice to save them.

"No." He gasped and dropped the barrier.

The outcry from her son seemed to center her because the red in her eyes faded. Frafnar spread his arms and sensed the existence of every magic missile aimed at them. He slapped his hands together and they all merged into one large projectile.

Sera straightened as if a great weight had left her shoulders.

"Gritt," she said with a sigh. "How can you—when?"

Clearly perplexed at losing control of her magic, the demose grasped futilely to regain it.

Frafnar bent his arms at the elbow and cupped his hands together above his chest. With all he had, he pushed his arms out. The hijacked magic swung around and careened back at its maker. The woman screamed when the missile hit her barrier, the explosion so bright that Frafnar flinched. A shockwave of heat and energy replaced the cool wind, and Sera yelled.

"We're too close!"

32

THE PROMISE

The world was crushing him, literally this time. Broken stone smothered Armastus, so heavy he could barely move. He sucked in a fraction of a breath. Pebbles and sand fell as he wiggled and pushed, sifting through the blanket of stone.

Another explosion rocked the soil, the sound muffled by his prison but clear enough. Sharp pointed edges dug into his arms, but his efforts were rewarded when his hand felt open air. He worked his way free of that stone coffin and staggered to his feet, battered and bruised. Blood flowed from cuts and mixed with the layers of dust on his skin.

Mounds of rubble covered the place, like dunes in a desert. It took Armastus a moment to orientate himself, but the pattern of the debris field made it obvious where the blast had originated.

Sera, he thought. That's where she'd be, and if not, it would be his final resting place if the demose still breathed. No crimsons crossed his path, probably avoiding their master for now. Any creature with a brain wouldn't venture into a place where such an explosion had occurred—a place so dangerous that the very ground was torn, and yet Armastus headed straight for it.

He only stopped to pull out a couple of grays from the rubble, sending the survivors to the Hole. Encounters became few and far between as he pressed on, ever closer to the core of the devastation.

Smoke seeped back into the air that the blast had cleared. Fires dotted the wreckage and filled the area with a dirty golden glow. Armastus crested a final mound when the crater came into view. The cobblestones were stripped away to reveal scraped dirt. Black-tinged fire swirled upward like a tornado, but stood still as a pillar, suggesting it might last forever to mark the battle.

Armastus saw Sera lying on her side. Her chest rose and fell, but the soil beneath her was wet and dark.

"Frafnar," she called as her mate neared, her eyes fluttering in his direction.

"He's not here," Armastus answered, kneeling next to her.

She sucked in a sharp breath, groaning. "He was. Did he make it?"

Armastus saw Erik arrive with his head down, glancing around nervously. The man found Frafnar's body and nodded to Armastus after a quick inspection.

"He's alive," Armastus said while visually tracing the thick splinters of the broken shield in her singed back. "But unconscious."

The pieces of wood and the heat of the explosion had

slowed her bleeding wounds, but her life still trickled into the soil.

"Good." She sighed and slid her dagger from her belt. An agonized groan escaped her lips, but she placed the weapon in his hands.

Armastus glowered, understanding the implication. "I'm not going anywhere."

"Get him to safety," Sera said as though she hadn't heard him. A tear escaped the corner of her eye. "Promise me. You can't die here. We both can't leave him."

When he refused to answer he could feel the fear in her fingers as they dug into his arm.

"Please."

Armastus clenched his jaw. Sera's hand slid over his and rested there.

"Please," she said again, her strength draining away.

It felt like an eternity while Armastus wrestled with the decision. His insides churned, and he wanted to rage at the world, but he remained rooted in place, staring at Sera's pleading face. How could he leave her? Frafnar would be fine.

The pain in her eyes settled his rage, calmed him until all the heat of anger was stone cold. He released a breath and his resolve shattered.

"I will."

33

FINALE

Armastus lifted Frafnar and curled his son's body over his shoulder, grasping his legs with the opposite arm. Sera watched him, relief radiating from her almost like a light in the dark, blossoming so bright it hurt to look. But he did, absorbing these last moments with his mate, no matter how much it pained him.

Erik's shoulders slumped after he examined Sera for himself. She couldn't move, and blood continued to moisten the soil. He gave her a drink from a vial.

"Go," she said softly. "I don't know how long..."

Erik took her hand and kissed it. When he stood, the light from the swirling pillar of fire glinted off the tears in his eyes. The man passed Armastus, who stood like stone.

"Go," she said again.

Armastus turned, but it took all he had to move away from her. Leaving her felt like a betrayal. Each step tore at his insides, shredding the heart she'd unearthed in him.

He imagined handing Frafnar over to Erik and returning to her side, but envisioning her sorrow destroyed his will.

Armastus shifted Frafnar's weight that now would be his alone to bear. Then he ran. Sera suffered every moment she held on for them.

Armastus and Erik, with an unconscious Frafnar, halted behind the mound of rubble closest to the Hole. A bubble of light surrounded it, and when any crimson dared get too close a streak of lightning would shoot out and send the orc flying back. The magic wouldn't kill them but was enough to repel them.

A crowd of crimsons made sport of it, to see who could get the closest and who would be thrown back the farthest. The gathering cheered and laughed when the current contender was flung clear over a wall. Armastus spotted Dejara inside the barrier and caught her eye.

"Is that all you've got?" she mocked the group. "Pathetic sucklings. Eager to bet against others when you're too cowardly to try." She followed her words with a few rude gestures.

The crimsons glanced at each other, clearly ready to shut her up. They pushed and shoved one another until the gathering was riled up enough—with continued prodding from Dejara—and charged together. Perhaps they hoped the magic couldn't repel so many, and they roared in triumph when nothing happened at first. They made it closer than any had before, but they were still a half dozen feet from the bubble when the biggest lightning bolt sizzled between them and sent them all flying.

Armastus and Erik dashed to the Hole. No lightning threatened them, not even a hint of static. Erik barreled through the magic while Armastus hesitated. He stepped over the threshold. The magic washed over him, and he could have sworn he felt Sera's hands lovingly caress his face before disappearing like vapor. It was tied to her life, but was it just his imagination?

It was a question he pondered as he delved into the Hole, away from the light and into the darkness.

"Sera?" Dejara called after him, but Erik answered her as he shook his head.

His words were lost in the echoes against the tunnel walls as Armastus kicked a support beam, Frafnar still on his shoulder. He put all his rage into that kick, and the beam never stood a chance.

EPILOGUE

The pillar of black-tinged fire abated, and a kneeling figure appeared through the flames. Valrix rose and stepped across the edge of the circle seared into the dirt. From time to time demonic power was required to save her. In this instance, it was a surprise.

"Still alive?" Valrix asked, circling Sera.

"Not for long," the Pale Witch replied softly.

"Indeed not." Valrix sensed the faint trace of magic. "Whatever you're doing won't work. Even in defeat, you struggle."

"If even one gray has the will to defy you... we've won."

"If this is victory"—Valrix spread her arms, embracing the carnage—"then defeat must be spectacular." She sighed. "But arguing with the dead is pointless. Tell me of the runt, and your suffering will end. How can an orc command gritt? He's your offspring?"

"You won't have him." An edge had entered Sera's voice,

but all her clout was spent in those few words, for she continued barely above a whisper. "He's gone."

The ground trembled beneath Valrix, and she stumbled as water sprayed up from the wreckage. The mist from a geyser clung to her as she seethed. "I'll hunt him down. I'll hunt them all down, do you hear me?" She spun toward the human, ready to kick her for a response, then stopped.

"Dead... already? How disappointing."

Valrix snapped her fingers, and flames engulfed the corpse, who had the faintest smile on her lips. Fitting that her ashes now mixed with those of her failed uprising. Valrix gaze turned to the burning ruins of Hammerstone while wolves howled in the distance.

"Rest assured; they won't escape me so easily."

ENCORE

THE OLD MAN

Some may wonder what became of the old man and his stubborn mule. Only he knew the trials of trying to get Betty to leave the tunnel. One look at the turbulent waters at the base of a waterfall locked the creature's legs stiff. No matter how he complained, threatened, pleaded, or pushed, Betty would not budge.

Another quake had the man peering into the dark tunnel apprehensively beyond the light of his torch. Betty attempted another kick, thinking he was still trying another push. He smacked her rump, not hard at all, and told her he wasn't.

The sound of footsteps grew louder and bounced off the stone walls, accompanied by a rumble that made the hairs on the back of his neck stand on end. The man was renewing his efforts with his mule when a trio bounded toward him, water lapping at their heels. Even poor Betty couldn't withstand the forces of nature, and all tumbled into the river.

The man thought he'd glimpsed a fourth figure slung over one of them before his torch extinguished with a hiss, but then the water enveloped him, and he could only pray one of Betty's hooves didn't find his noggin in the chaos beneath the surface.

His sons had been right about one thing. He'd be sure to tell them of the greatest adventure he'd had in years. If he survived...

THANK YOU!

Thank you for your interest in *Blood Branded*. It's nice to know some people love fantasy as much as I do, and I hope you enjoyed it.

I'd love to know your thoughts!

If you have a moment, please consider leaving a review on:
Amazon or **Goodreads**

Why write a review?

It helps other readers know if the story is something they'd enjoy. It also helps authors understand the preferences of their readers. This is useful when developing great stories.

Both the good and bad, let us know. We thank you in advance. You rock!

KNIGHTS OF MYTHRETH: BOOK ONE

THE KNIGHT'S ORDER

J·A·ALEXSOO

ABOUT J.A. ALEXSOO

J.A. Alexsoo lives in Ontario, Canada, and has forever been a fan of fantasy and science fiction. When not working on writing or imagining new adventures, she tours the lands with her three trusty canine companions.

For more, visit:
www.JAAlexsoo.com/about

AUTHOR'S NOTE

Would you believe that *Blood Branded* was supposed to be a two-thousand-word short story? It's not a huge stretch from a small novella, but it seems Frafnar's tale had more to it than I'd anticipated. There are two more books planned for readers hoping that the story continues.

I wrote this after *The Knight's Order* to better understand Frafnar's hatred of crimsons, and for those who liked the character and were curious about his origins. He's becoming a favorite of mine too.

Thank you, dear readers, for your interest and your time. I hope I did this tale the justice it deserves and that it was enjoyable. I'm always trying to think about what kind of extras I could share about my stories and the realms of Mythreth, so if you have any suggestions, please let me know through my website.

I'd also like to thank my beta readers for their tremendous help polishing the rough edges. Your input is invaluable and greatly appreciated.

And a special thank you to:

David Antrobus – **EDITOR**
Hugh Pindur – **COVER DESIGNER**
Tad Davis – **MAP ILLUSTRATOR**

You guys are amazing!

September 2019
J.A. Alexsoo

WWW. JAALEXSOO.COM

If you want exclusive content, behind the scene adventures, information about J.A. Alexsoo's next novel, or other topics for readers and fantasy fans, you can **sign up for her newsletter**. Your email will remain confidential and you can unsubscribe anytime.
www. JAAlexsoo.com/newsletter

Found a typo?
Oh no! Every book has at least one typo and we want to make our book as perfect as possible.
{*Merriam-Webster's Collegiate Dictionary, 11th ed.*}
{**Note:** See **Glossary** for unique spelling.}
Let us know at:
www. JAAlexsoo.com/contact-me

GLOSSARY

(the) Avant Guard—An order of talented knights with gritt who keep peace in the realms. Also known as the Order. Some call them Ordained.

crimson orcs—They are the most ruthless, temperamental, unreasonable, and violent of the orcs. Before the rule of the demose, all was chaos.

demose—Demons who fight for domination of Mythreth, commonly using mortals to get a foothold into it. They are attracted to power and revel in death and destruction. They each have their own desires and will destroy other demose if they get in the way of their plans. When they succeed in merging with the mortals of Mythreth, their consciousness takes over.

grayback orcs—Also known as grays, their society lives

under the thumb of their crimson cousins, an outcome of wars long past. Some grays rebel for independence and freedom, but none have been successful so far. They are more reasonable than their crimson cousins.

gritt—A talent with the power to manipulate and control other magic. All members of the Avant Guard have this ability, at different skill levels. Remnents also have this ability.

Hammerstone—The first grayback settlement to oppose the crimson orcs.

mix-blood—Those whose heritage is of more than one race. Also known as a half-breed.

orcs—They are the descendants of ancient humans who revered the demose. These humans relied on the demose for so long that it permanently changed their physical appearance. Eventually their descendants were immune to the coercion and could no longer merge with demons. They remain larger and stronger than their modern human counterparts and have a high resistance to magic.

(the) Order—Also known as the Avant Guard Order.

Remnents—People who are gifted with gritt and are possessed by a demon.

rune—A magic circle of any size, infused with arcane symbols.

runts—Orc children and young orcs.

suckling—An insult toward crimson orcs, a word associating the color of their skin to newborns.

twig—An orc insult meaning weak and useless.

www.ingramcontent.com/pod-product-compliance
Lightning Source LLC
Chambersburg PA
CBHW051927110726
47902CB00002B/448